MarShmallOw
Pie the Cat SuPerstar
⇒ on TV ⇐

Marshmallow Pie the Cat Superstar on TV

Clara Vulliamy

HarperCollins *Children's Books*

First published in Great Britain by
HarperCollins *Children's Books* in 2020
HarperCollins *Children's Books* is a division of HarperCollins*Publishers* Ltd,
HarperCollins Publishers
1 London Bridge Street
London SE1 9GF

The HarperCollins website address is
www.harpercollins.co.uk

1

ISBN 978-0-00-835589-0

Printed and bound in England by CPI Group (UK) Ltd, Croydon CR0 4YY

MIX
Paper from
responsible sources
FSC™ C007454

For Angela, with love

Map of the TV studio

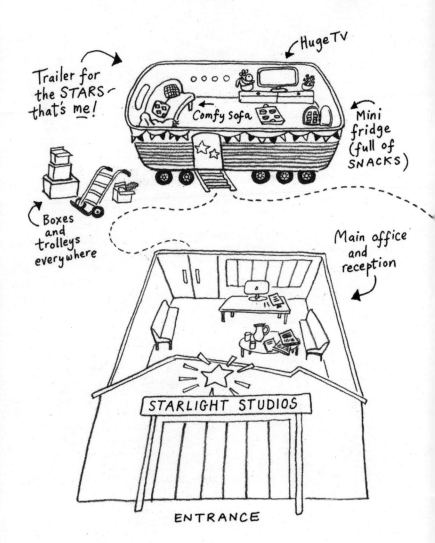

Huge TV

Trailer for the STARS - that's me!

Comfy sofa

Mini fridge (full of SNACKS)

Boxes and trolleys everywhere

Main office and reception

STARLIGHT STUDIOS

ENTRANCE

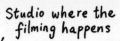
Studio where the filming happens

The 'little house' set

Waiting area

Director's chair and loudspeaker

Expensive lights and cameras

SILENCE SILENCE

tasty smells!

ERNIE'S EATS

Catering truck

Ladders, scenery, MORE boxes

Make-up and hair-stylist's trailer (where I become EVEN MORE gorgeous and fluffy)

Chapter One
Fluffy and Fabulous

Oh, hello. Yes, yes – it IS me. You
probably recognise me . . .

Marshmallow Pie. *Actor. Celebrity.
Superstar.*

And here's the proof: my first-ever acting job, an advert for Snow White washing powder.

It's been published at last. It feels like *ages* since I was at the photographer's studio having my picture taken.

I must say I was pretty awesome. All I had to do was sit there under the spotlights, the centre of attention, with a constant supply of amazing snacks. Everyone said they had literally never seen a cat so fluffy and fabulous.

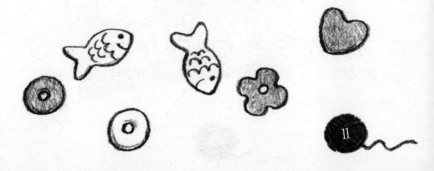

Amelia, my human, has
picked up one or two copies.

'Are you sure you have enough?' her dad
asks, chuckling. 'There's still a LITTLE
bit of bare wall, just here . . .'

'Oh, but I'm SO proud of Pie!' she
replies. 'I might get just a *few* more.'

It's a warm summery morning and the balcony door is open. I wander outside to sit in the sun for a while. I'm also hoping that Buster is out on his balcony too.

Buster lives in the flat below. Ever since he got the job of advertising **Beefy Chews** dog food he thinks *he's* a star, but he needs to watch out for the competition.

Yes, he's there. I can hear him, snuffling and slobbering.

I press my face through the railings and, oh dear, I *accidentally* drop my copy of the Snow White advert. It floats gently down to the balcony below and lands on Buster.

He responds with a commotion of crazy barking. Totally jealous.

I come in from the balcony and hop up on to Amelia's lap for a nice head-scratch and a cuddle. Amelia and her dad are chatting together while they have their lunch.

'At school we've been given a creative-writing project to do over the holidays,' she is telling him, 'and I was wondering about setting up a school newspaper for animal and pet news – if I feel brave enough.'

What, OTHER animals and pets apart from *me*? Sounds very dull.

But her dad says, 'That's a brilliant idea! Pie's Snow White advert could be on the front page!'

Ah, well, *now* you're talking. The world needs to hear about my incredible talents.

'It could be a very good way to make friends,' he carries on.

'Yes, maybe,' she agrees, going a bit *pink*. 'I'll think about it. If I do, I'm going to call it the ***Fluffington Post***.'

After lunch, while Amelia helps her dad with the hoovering, I find a comfy cushion in a warm spot. It's important to have at least *twenty* proper naps each day, with several small snoozes in between.

I take relaxing very seriously and will not move until I've rested enough. Amelia has to hoover around me.

I think I must have dozed off, because the sound of the telephone ringing in the kitchen wakes me up. I can just make out Dexter's voice. He's my agent from the Ace Animal Acting Agency.

He is saying to Amelia, 'I have some **EXCITING NEWS** ...'

Chapter Two
Mini Crunchlets

'Pie, PIE!' Amelia puts down the phone and rushes into the room. 'A **BIG** job has come in for you – in a TV advert!'

I act casual, barely opening my eyes. It's no surprise to me. After the washing-powder triumph I was bound to become a superstar in no time.

'It's for the company who make **Shrimp Crunchies**,' Amelia says.

I can't help my tongue popping out a little bit. **Shrimp Crunchies** are my absolute favourite.

'They are launching a new range of smaller biscuits for kittens, called **Mini Crunchlets**.'

Wait. **Shrimp Crunchies**, but SMALL? What's the point of that?

I have to tell you, I am NOT a fan of kittens. Cheeky, pouncing on my tail, no respect for their elders. And I've met enough to know . . . All right, only one, but that was *plenty*. I'm keeping well away from kittens.

Meanwhile, Amelia is beside herself with excitement. 'You're going to be a **HUGE** star, Pie!' she says. '*Nothing* can stand in your way now!'

I let her carry on like this, although to be quite honest I'm a huge star already.

'We need to get you looking your absolute best for TV,' she tells me. 'I'm just going to pop out to buy some new grooming supplies from **Pawsitively Purrfect**. I won't be long.'

Amelia leaves me watching *Woodland Birds* on the iPad. I bat at the birds with my paw, but I never seem to catch one. Instead a very handsome cat appears.

My Accidental iPad Selfies

When Amelia gets back, she has more news.

'I just bumped into Zack from school and his kitten, Gingernut,' she says.

I feel instantly uneasy. You remember I told you about the kitten I met? Put me off for life? Well, that was her. Gingernut.

'And *guess what?*' Amelia carries on, all smiles. 'Gingernut will be your co-star in the **Mini Crunchlets** advert!'

I am **APPALLED**. To find out I will be sharing the spotlight AT ALL is bad enough, but with *that* naughty kitten? Seriously? It's *unbelievable.*

I'm still absolutely reeling from this news when Amelia makes a further terrible announcement.

'Now,' she says, taking a bottle of cat shampoo out of her bag, 'for the first part of your special makeover, you're going to have . . . A BATH!'

There is literally nothing in the world I hate more than a bath. It's **SO** embarrassing. I insist that you look away *right now*.

Amelia is chatting about how thrilling it all is. 'Just think – you'll be ON TV! I can hardly believe it!'

I don't react. I'm too busy trying to **shake** the water out of my fur.

'And another thing,' she adds, gently brushing me, 'Zack is really keen to be involved with my school newspaper idea. So it's decided – we're going to set up the *Fluffington Post* together!'

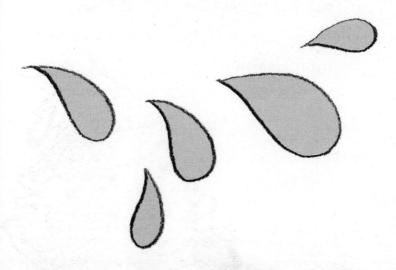

Chapter Three

First Rule of Showbiz:
Be Cool, Like Me

On the morning of our first day at the film studio, Amelia's dad gives us a lift.

'I am SO NERVOUS!' says Amelia. 'I hardly slept a wink!'

As we pull up outside, we press our noses to the car window and see busy-looking people rushing in and out of the gleaming glass doors.

'Have fun!' says Amelia's dad. 'See you later!'

Amelia takes a deep breath, and we
go inside. She seems shy and a little
overwhelmed to be here, but I feel I
belong.

Zack has arrived already and is waiting
for us in reception. Amelia smiles with
relief to see him.

And there's Gingernut. Bouncing around the room like a little orange baked bean on springs. Climbing up everything, including people. *Far* too friendly with everyone. When she sees me she is **SO EXCITED** – running round and round me, a maddening blur. *TOO KEEN*, I think to myself. The first rule of showbiz: be cool, like me.

'As this is Gingernut's very first job and Pie is much more experienced,' Zack says, 'he'll be able to teach her everything she needs to know.'

Well, that's where they're wrong. You can't teach raw talent like mine. You either have it or you don't.

A young woman with a headset and clipboard hurries over to us. 'Hi! I'm Darcy. I'll be looking after you while you're here. First let's get you settled in to your trailer – follow me, please!'

We weave in and out of people carrying boxes and pushing trolleys, shouting over to other people lifting equipment and pulling scenery.

In our trailer we find exactly the kind of luxury a star like me should expect. There are two pink velvet sofas piled high with soft cushions and blankets, overflowing food bowls on a fancy tray and a mini fridge with a tantalising glimpse of yet more delicious food inside.

'Wow!' says Amelia.

'It's amazing!' agrees Zack.

Darcy notices me looking. 'Fancy a snack?' she says. I already like this woman. 'You can help yourself whenever you want.'

I like her a LOT.

The only thing I *don't* like is that I have
to share the trailer with Gingernut.

'And now I'll take you on a tour of the studio,' says Darcy.

She shows us the make-up and hair-stylist's trailer. 'Or in your case *fur* stylist, of course!' says Darcy. 'You'll come here to get ready.'

Then we go past the catering truck, from which tasty, spicy smells are wafting over, mixed with the strong scent of coffee.

Amelia and Zack are both jotting things down in their notebooks. 'This would make a brilliant article for the **Fluffington Post**,' says Amelia. 'All about the wonderful world of the TV studio!'

CATS ON TV!
At the studio the stars have their own trailer.
It's amazing!!
HUGE TV!
Unlimited snacks (for cats and humans)!!!

'Cool!' says Darcy. 'I'm still at college and only working here for a few weeks, but ask me anything you want to know. I love it *all* – the sights, the sounds . . . SO exciting! But look, here comes the director, Brad Carter.'

A tall blond man in a white suit strides past.

Darcy tries to attract his attention. 'May I introduce your cat actors, Mr Carter?' she begins.

He glances in our direction but barely acknowledges us. 'I DON'T HAVE TIME!' he calls over his shoulder, waving a hand dismissively.

How *rude*.

'I've worked on all the GREAT television,' we hear him proclaiming loudly to a camerawoman as they walk away, 'but **Mini Crunchlets** will be my *masterpiece.*'

'He can be a bit offhand,' whispers Darcy, when he's gone.

'He also seems a bit . . . vain?' Amelia whispers back.

'Yes – what a fake tan!' adds Zack.

The three of them try – and fail – to hide their giggles.

I don't know what a fake tan is. It might have something to do with the fact that Brad Carter is practically as orange as Gingernut.

Chapter Four
Take One – ACTION!

We get ready to start filming. Darcy takes us over to the make-up and hair-stylist's trailer.

Amelia and Zack lift me and Gingernut up on to high stools in front of a large mirror with lights all round it.

'All you both need is a little light brushing,' the stylist says. Turning to me he adds, 'And extra fluffy ear tufts for you, big fella!'

Big fella. *I LOVE* that.

I look at my reflection and think, *WHO IS THAT HANDSOME CAT?* Why, yes, it's *me*, of course.

Then we go on to the set itself. It's very noisy and very busy. Some people are hammering in nails, others rushing past with pots of paint, and there's filming equipment everywhere – cameras, fancy lights, cables, screens . . .

Gingernut and I are both startled to see something fluffy, grey and catlike poking out from under a chair.

Gingernut **meows** a *friendly* hello and I give it a **grumpy** growl. TWO co-stars?

Absolutely not!

Out of the question.

Then somebody picks it up and speaks into it.

'Testing, testing . . .'

But OF COURSE I knew it was a microphone. I definitely DID NOT think it was another cat. Only Gingernut did. Anyone who suggests I thought so too is utterly mistaken.

Then Brad the director sweeps in, and we all gather round him while he shows us what will happen in the advert.

'It's an idyllic family scene,' Brad tells us. 'A big cat is looking after his small kitten.'

Sigh. I do NOT want to look after a small kitten, even in an advert.

The scenery is a little house made of wooden board, everything in miniature so it's just the right size for us.

There is a catflap decorated to look like a front door, and pretty curtains framing a paper window painted with fluffy white clouds. On a low table there are two expensive-looking china bowls (one big and one small), a large jug of milk and a box of **Mini Crunchlets**.

Amelia notices a little
rucksack for Gingernut,
hanging on a peg. 'Look,
Zack,' she says, 'there are
tiny schoolbooks inside!'

'All you have to do,' Brad says, turning to me and Gingernut, 'is come in from the side, meOW excitedly and walk over to the kitchen table. The big cat serves breakfast by pressing this button *here*, which tips the box of **Crunchlets** into the kitten's bowl. After eating breakfast the kitten picks up her rucksack and trots out through the catflap as if going to school.'

Sounds almost TOO easy.

'Then the human voice-over will say . . .'

The sound engineer turns a dial on her computer.

'I give my darling kitten a bowl of **Mini Crunchlets** *— the* purrfect *way to start the day.'*

We have a few minutes to get ready. I rehearse one of my *best* moves, which is my swaggering walk. Gingernut tries to copy me.

I find copycats VERY irritating. I hiss at
Gingernut to make her stop stealing my
moves. She should find her *own* things
to do.

'Okay, TAKE YOUR POSITIONS!' calls
Brad. 'And . . . take one – ACTION!'

When the cameras start
filming, Gingernut
does do her own
thing. She hops up
on to her back legs
and sniffs the air,
as if smelling the
tasty **Crunchlets**.

Now, I KNOW what I said about copycats. But this is different, because *I* am the senior star here and this move would definitely look better coming from me. Standing in front of Gingernut, I puff up my magnificent fluffiness, hop up on to my back legs and sniff the air, as if smelling the tasty **Crunchlets.** Yes, I am an acting genius.

'CUT!' calls out Brad, annoyed. 'Cute moves from the big cat but I can't even SEE the kitten. She needs to do better – right now she has no stage presence WHATSOEVER.'

Gingernut goes a bit quiet. Oh dear. Perhaps I got a *little* carried away.

But now the *highlight* of the day – everything stops for lunch.

Chapter Five

Who's the Buffoon Around Here, Exactly?

After lunch Gingernut and I just lounge in our trailer. There's a great selection of toys here. Gingernut particularly loves the cuddly fish with a bell inside.

Amelia and Zack go off to get themselves some warm cheese toasties from the catering truck, and Darcy has some jobs to do.

She is sorting through a big box of pet costumes, deciding what to keep and what to throw away. I think I can help with this – my judgement on style is absolutely the BEST.

I try on a carnival hat.

'FRUITY!' says Darcy admiringly.

Then I try a tiny crown, a wizard hat and a sparkly necklace. I put on a feather boa too, but it tickles my nose.

Feline Groovy

Then Gingernut and I both try on snowman outfits, although to be honest you need a belly like mine to *really* do it justice.

Back on set, Darcy suggests some vocal warm-ups for our meows.

Gingernut's meow is rather small. It gets drowned out by mine, which is IMMENSE. Why do they need a human voice-over when they could have ME?

We start filming again. I must admit I do love being a superstar. I'm dazzled for a moment by my own marvellousness – everybody looking at me, the lights, the cameras, the glory . . . ! I'm imagining crowds cheering, prizes being awarded, my name up in lights . . .

Then I come back to earth with a jolt,
to find Gingernut nudging me urgently.
I'd forgotten my cue to press the button
that tips the box of **Crunchlets**. I
hastily press it *just* in time.

Gingernut eats up her 'breakfast',
and I give her a quick nuzzle goodbye
(because I am playing the part of a
loving parent, after all). Then it's time
for her big moment.

She goes to pick up the little
rucksack . . . but it's GONE!

Gingernut stops in her
tracks, uncertain what
to do. A tense few
seconds pass.

'CUT!' shouts Brad, exasperated. He throws his arms up in the air in fury. 'How many times are we going to need to film this scene? I can't work with these **BUFFOONS!**'

Well, I think *that's* a bit harsh. And anyway, I'M not a buffoon – I performed *my* role. I glance over at Gingernut, who's standing there looking small and worried.

Everyone is frantically looking for the rucksack, and Gingernut joins in the search. She looks embarrassed, like she thinks it must be her fault. It's a shame, but I let them get on with it and give myself a quick groom, paying particular attention to fluffing up my glorious tail. It's important that I'm always looking good.

Darcy finally finds the rucksack . . .
underneath me.

Oops. I didn't realise I'd been sitting on
it all along.

Gingernut's ears droop miserably.

'Now we've run out of time,'
storms Brad. 'What a waste of
a day!'

He stomps off in a huff. We
can hear him shouting all
the way across the studio.

'This is MY masterpiece
and I am surrounded by
idiots!'

Darcy runs after him with
his messenger bag. 'Wait,
Mr Carter – you forgot this!'

He takes it but
doesn't even say
thank you.

Darcy starts packing away the props
until tomorrow. 'We're all doing our
best,' she says quietly.

'What a RUDE man,' says Amelia, and
Zack agrees.

Chapter Six
An Absolute LEGEND

It's day two at the studio, and the filming carries on. There's an awful lot of waiting and hanging around. Luckily the mini fridge is kept well stocked.

In a break between takes, Brad is in deep conversation with the camerawoman, and we are sitting just to one side of our little house, waiting to get started again.

Gingernut brings me her favourite cuddly fish toy with a friendly meoW, hoping to play. But I'm just not in the mood – I need to catch up on my daily number of naps and snoozes. She gives up trying and huddles in the corner instead.

Zack takes Gingernut with him to the catering truck. I have a little sleep while Amelia does some writing in her **Fluffington Post** notebook.

A little while later I wake up, starving as usual, and find to my delight that there are two boxes of chicken and bacon from the catering truck waiting for me. How generous of them to give me TWO helpings!

MARSHMALLOW PIE

GINGERNUT

Darcy is just giving Gingernut a last brush nearby in the little house, which means filming is about to begin again. I quickly gobble up the snacks while I have the chance.

'Oh NO, Pie!' gasps Amelia, looking up from her notebook. 'One of those special treats was for Gingernut!'

Gingernut turns round. She stares in disbelief at the empty boxes. This time she is not just disappointed. She is **CROSS.**

She leaps off Darcy's lap, stamps her little paws and tries to leave, but in her haste she trips over the rucksack.

She stumbles, staggers
and falls against the table . . .
and the big jug of milk
perched on the edge falls
to the floor with a

CRASH.

Milk floods out of the smashed jug, all over an expensive camera. It spreads across the floor to one of the plug sockets. There's an ominous fizzing sound and one of the fancy lights goes out.

Darcy, Zack and Amelia see the damage and are frozen to the spot with horror.

Then Brad sees it too.

He marches across and towers over Gingernut. She is standing in a milky puddle, trembling with fear.

'The jug, the camera, the light – all **RUINED!**' he yells at her. 'YOU ARE A COMPLETE **DISASTER!**'

I look at Gingernut's shocked, scared little face.

This is TOO MUCH.

I find myself hissing **FURIOUSLY** at Brad for being so MEAN. It was just an accident. Hasn't Gingernut always tried her best?

But
    then
        I
            start
                thinking . . .

She's always tried her best to be kind to me too. But have I been kind in return, or have I just made everything worse?

The cute move to hop up
on to our back legs and
sniff the air was HER
idea. But I took over

and blocked
her from view,
so she never
got the credit.

And wasn't she trying
to help me, when she
reminded me to press the
Crunchlets button? But instead of

being grateful, all I did was ruin her big moment by sitting on her rucksack. I should have been more careful.

Despite all of this, she still wanted to play with me. She even offered me her favourite toy, but I ignored her. And then I went and ate her special box of treats without thinking.

I see I have been a bit selfish. I didn't want to play the role of her loving parent on TV, but I admit that maybe I DO feel protective towards her after all. Taking care of a small kitten isn't about silly, fake things like pouring them their breakfast in an advert. It's about standing up for them when they need you.

I look meaningfully at Amelia, and she looks back at me. She understands. The only way I can make it up to Gingernut is to draw attention away from her milk-jug accident by doing something much, MUCH worse.

My Coolest Moves EVER

I jump up on to the table – sending **Mini Crunchlets** flying through the air – and backflip against the wall of the little wooden house, causing it to wobble dangerously. Then, in one tremendous leap, I dive headfirst towards the paper window and burst through the fluffy white clouds.

As I land on the other side, the little house comes toppling down, piece by piece. The back wall falls towards me, but I'm prepared. I sit perfectly in line with the broken paper window, and it frames me neatly as the wall crashes to the ground.

I am an absolute *LEGEND*.

'ARGH! MY MASTERPIECE!'
explodes Brad.
'DESTROYED!'

There is a shocked
silence, except for
the sound of **Mini
Crunchlets** landing on
the floor.

All that remains is the
table and on it my large
expensive china bowl. I
have one final move up
my sleeve.

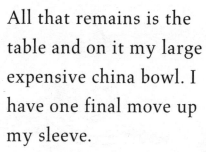

I stroll up to the table. I look straight at Brad, fixing him with a beady stare, and tap the bowl towards the table's edge.

Tap, tap . . .

Everyone is holding their breath, looking at me, then at him, then back at me again.

Tap, tap, tap . . .

Brad stares, his eyes bulging with fury.
I nudge the bowl closer, closer, closer to
the edge . . .

. . . until it falls off
the table and smashes
satisfyingly into a
hundred pieces on
the floor.

At that moment, the smoking milk-soaked plug socket causes the sprinklers to come on. It is raining heavily, *indoors*.

Brad is SOAKED, orange-streaked water dripping down his face and on to his white jacket. At first he can't speak, only splutter.

'YOU ARE BOTH FIRED!' he roars,

when he gets his voice back. **'YOU WILL NEVER WORK AGAIN!'**

'Let's get out of here, Pie,' says Amelia. 'We don't want to work with someone like that anyway.'

'Absolutely,' agrees Zack. 'Let's go, Gingernut!'

Amelia, Zack, Gingernut and I walk out, heads held high.

Out of the corner of my eye I see Darcy holding up her phone.

Chapter Seven
Friends, Flakes and Family

'That moment when Pie *literally* brought the house down,' Zack is saying, 'I couldn't believe it! And taking the heat off Gingernut like that – he was INCREDIBLE!'

'Yes, he WAS!' agrees Amelia, going pink and smiling. 'And Gingernut was brilliant too. She tried SO hard to be a good co-star.'

The four of us are sitting in the park. We don't feel like going home just yet.

Gingernut and I are in a very good mood. We roll on the grass, examine a buttercup, watch a bee fly past. We aren't at all bothered about being fired from the TV advert. In fact, it was all pretty hilarious.

'And wasn't Brad awful?' Amelia carries on. 'He really deserved to be taken down a peg or two.'

'He was terrible!' says Zack. 'It was SO funny when the sprinklers came on and his fake tan washed off.'

Amelia laughs. 'We have LOTS of material for our **Fluffington Post** article,' she says. 'Let's call it "The highs and lows of life in showbiz"!'

They chat about it some more, but the

bee has come back so Gingernut and I are too busy to listen. We chase the bee for a while, until I am all puffed out. I allow Gingernut to pounce on my tail a LITTLE bit. (I do understand – it's just too gorgeous to resist.)

When it's finally time to wander slowly back, we call in at **Pawsitively Purrfect** to buy some kitty litter for Gingernut.

There, taped up on the window in among the pet food and toys, is a poster of somebody I know only too well.

BUSTER.

'Oh, look!' says Amelia. 'It says here that Buster is the local *celebrity* who will be opening the new shopping centre next month.'

Meet local celebrity **BUSTER** at the grand opening of **SPRINGFIELD SHOPPING CENTRE!**

'It seems his career is taking off,' says Zack.

'Seems so, yes,' agrees Amelia in a quiet voice. 'Oh well.'

It's extremely irritating to see Buster's annoying face again. But I don't dwell on it for long. I have *much* more important things to think about . . . because next we are stopping off at the kiosk, and sometimes that means TREATS FOR ME.

Amelia and Zack buy ice creams at the kiosk. The kind lady who works there gives them an extra chocolate flake in their cones.

We say goodbye to Zack and Gingernut.
'See you tomorrow!' calls out Zack, and
Amelia waves back.

'So,' says Amelia as she carries me home,
'I suppose our dreams of you being on
TV are all over.'

I give her a little head-boop, to show her
I understand. We're family. I don't like
to see her feeling disappointed.

'But you did the right thing, Pie,' she adds. 'Friends come first.'

And she gives me a little lick of her ice cream.

Chapter Eight
Global SENSATION –
That's Me!

The next morning I am taking it easy, recovering from all my hard work over the last few days.

At this exact moment I'm sitting in the bathroom basin, drinking the drips from the tap. Amelia and her dad have to brush their teeth in the kitchen sink.

Later on Zack comes over, bringing
Gingernut with him. He and Amelia are
going to finish off their article for the
Fluffington Post, and they have arranged to
get together every two weeks to write more.

I have to make room for the **Fluffington
Post** HQ, which is actually the sofa.

'Gingernut is taking a break from
showbiz for a while,' Zack tells Amelia,
'to enjoy just being a kitten.'

'Sounds like a great idea,' says Amelia.

I give Gingernut a tour of my toybox, and where to find some good crumbs under the kitchen table. Then I take her outside on to the balcony and show her the sunniest spots to sit.

I also teach her how to annoy Buster with the tail-flick trick. We hang our tails down through the railings and give them a little wiggle to attract his attention. He can see us, but he can't reach. It drives him absolutely CRAZY.

She's a quick learner.

Oh, all right, then. I let her have a
cuddle too.

I'm still not sure about kittens . . . but
this one is okay.

Later that afternoon, when Zack and Gingernut have gone home, Amelia and I are curled up on the sofa, watching my new favourite programme on the iPad. It's called *Fish Tank Fun*.

'Hey – come and see this!' calls out her dad, pointing excitedly at something on his laptop. Amelia hurries over.

'It's PIE!' she exclaims. 'At the TV studio!' She pulls up a chair next to him.

'It was Darcy,' says Amelia. 'She must have videoed the whole catastrophe and put it on YouTube!'

I jump up on to her lap to see. It's even
better than watching *Fish Tank Fun*, and
that's saying *a lot*. I look

AMAZING.

Amelia and her dad carry on watching
together, as more and more people all
over the world are watching it too . . .

10,000 views . . . 100,000 . . .

Now climbing to half a million . . . now a million . . .

'This film clip is going viral!' says Amelia's dad. 'Pie is an internet sensation!'

The telephone rings. It's my agent, Dexter.

'A *huge* film producer in Hollywood has seen the video,' he tells Amelia, 'and thinks Pie will be *perfect* for the role of the villain cat in a major new movie!'

Amelia's eyes grow wide with astonishment. She can hardly utter a word, and just gives a joyful little squeak.

'Never mind the small screen,' Dexter carries on. 'The BIG screen awaits!'

Amelia's dad is shaking his head in absolute disbelief and laughing.

I take it all in my stride, though. I've spotted half a **Shrimp Crunchie** wedged under a chair leg, so I'm mainly concentrating on getting my paws on that.

But I am pleased that what seemed a disaster at the time turned out to be a triumph after all. It just goes to show – nothing can stand in the way of a HUGE talent like mine.

Amelia sweeps me up in her arms. 'We must pack our bags straight away,' she says . . .

'We're going to . . .

HOLLYWOOD!'

The End

Look out for Marshmallow Pie's next adventure – in Hollywood!

Marshmallow Pie the Cat Superstar in Hollywood

Clara Vulliamy

Do you know where Marshmallow Pie's path to stardom begins? Read on for a preview of his first story . . .

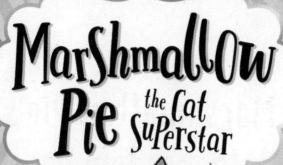

Marshmallow Pie the Cat Superstar

Clara Vulliamy

Chapter One

Marvellous Me

Oh, hello. Yes, you can come in, but you can't sit down because there's only room for me on this sofa.

I am a fancy cat. I prefer to be addressed by my FULL name, which is *Marshmallow Marmaduke Vanilla-Bean Sugar-Pie Fluffington-Fitz-Noodle.*

I'm not happy when people shorten it.

I pretend I haven't heard them, at first.

Here comes my human,
Amelia Lime.

'Hello, Pie!' she says. See what I have to put up with?

I live here with Amelia and her dad in a tiny top-floor flat in the middle of the busy city. I didn't always, though.

The Early Years

Until not long ago I lived in a huge
house in the country with Amelia's
rich Aunt Julia, until she jumped into
her private plane to fly around the
world and couldn't take me with her.
So I was popped into the back of a taxi
and sent over to Amelia. I would be
company for her, everyone said.

I like the easy life.

I spend a lot of time sitting in the
sunshine on our little balcony.

There's a dog called Buster in the flat below. When he is out on his balcony I look down on him, in every way, which drives him CRAZY and keeps me entertained for hours.

This afternoon Amelia throws down her school bag and excitedly rummages in her coat pocket. 'Look – just look at this!' she says, pulling out a conker, a broken pencil, a hair clip shaped like a space rocket and, finally, a crumpled piece of paper. I yawn, waiting for her to get to the point. 'They were giving out these leaflets in **Pawsitively Purrfect** when I went in to buy your Shrimp Crunchies . . .'

I can't help doing a little dribble. **Pawsitively Purrfect** is a very good pet shop, and Shrimp Crunchies are my favourite.

Amelia reads the leaflet aloud . . .

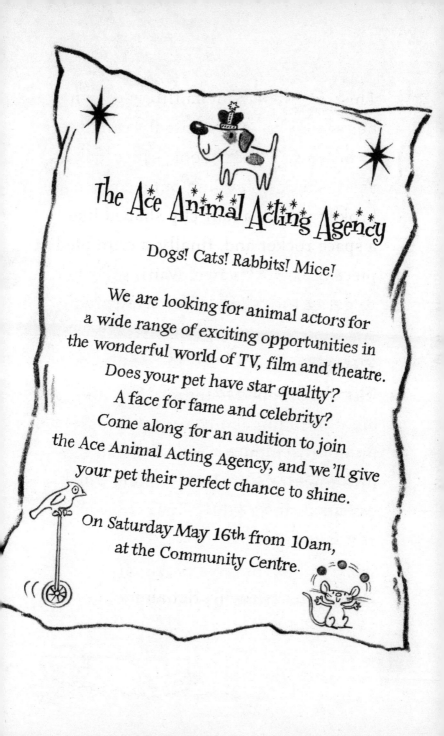

The Ace Animal Acting Agency

Dogs! Cats! Rabbits! Mice!

We are looking for animal actors for
a wide range of exciting opportunities in
the wonderful world of TV, film and theatre.
Does your pet have star quality?
A face for fame and celebrity?
Come along for an audition to join
the Ace Animal Acting Agency, and we'll give
your pet their perfect chance to shine.

On Saturday May 16th from 10am,
at the Community Centre.

'It's REALLY SOON, Pie – only one week's time! Pie?'

But I've stopped listening. I'm too busy thinking about my tea. I pick up my toy mouse, Squeaker, and I go into the kitchen where Amelia's dad is working at the table.

'Hey, kiddo,' he says to Amelia, looking up from his laptop. 'How was school?'

'Hey, Dad,' says Amelia. 'Usual stuff.'

I pace up and down impatiently while
Amelia sorts the **Shrimp Crunchies**
into my bowl. They come in yellow,
pink and white, but I will only eat the
yellow ones.

Amelia's dad is reading her school
newsletter while they eat their tea
together.

'Let's see if there's anything here you might like to do,' he says. 'Netball team try-outs?'

'I don't think so,' says Amelia.

'Twinkle Toes Dance Club?'

'No way!'

'Well, how about this – why don't you enter the public-speaking competition? You can do it in pairs, it says here.'

Amelia's cheeks go pink. 'Oh no, that would be the WORST,' she says.

'Everyone would be looking at me, and I wouldn't be able to find a partner to do it with anyway.'

She shows her dad the acting-agency leaflet. 'This is loads better. I'd still get to do exciting things, but it would be PIE in the spotlight, not me. Pie deserves to be a HUGE star and I'm going to help him!'

I only really hear the last bit, as I tend to zone out if the conversation isn't about me. A star? I feel like a star already, to be quite honest.

'We MUST give the acting audition a go,' Amelia carries on when I've finished my tea and I'm just giving

my whiskers a quick clean. 'They're
sure to give you a place in their
agency – they will love you!'

Of course they will. I lick a stray
crumb that has got stuck up my nose.
A class act, that's me.

While Amelia is brushing her teeth at bedtime, I jump up on to the edge of the bath and investigate an open bottle of shampoo.

'We need to make sure you're looking absolutely fantastic,' she says, 'and take photos, make a business card and begin your TRAINING! Lucky it's the weekend tomorrow, no school . . . We'll start first thing in the morning.'

I give the bottle a little tap with my paw.

'You will try your very best, won't you? Pie?'

I don't answer. I keep tapping the
shampoo until it falls on to the floor.

S
p
l
a
t.

NICE.

Find out what happens next inside *Marshmallow Pie the Cat Superstar!*

Check out more of Clara's books...

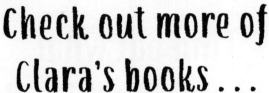